Wild Eggs

A Tale of Arctic Egg Collecting

Dedicated to my father, who took me out egg hunting and taught me the rules of Mother Nature.

Published by Inhabit Media Inc.
www.inhabitmedia.com

Inhabit Media Inc. (Iqaluit) P.O. Box 11125, Iqaluit, Nunavut, X0A 1H0
(Toronto) 146 A Orchard View Blvd., Toronto, Ontario, M4R 1C3

Edited by Louise Flaherty and Neil Christopher
Art Direction by Danny Christopher

We acknowledge the financial support of the Government of Canada through the Department of Canadian Heritage Canada Book Fund.

We acknowledge the support of the Canada Council for the Arts for our publishing program.

Printed in Canada.

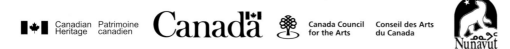

Library and Archives Canada Cataloguing in Publication

Napayok-Short, Suzie, 1959-, author
    Wild eggs : a tale of Arctic egg collecting / by Suzie Napayok-Short
; illustrated by Jonathan Wright.

ISBN 978-1-77227-025-9 (bound)

    I. Wright, Jonathan, 1978-, illustrator II. Title.

PS8627.A62 W55 2015   jC813'.6   C2015-904785-4

Wild Eggs
A Tale of Arctic Egg Collecting

By Suzie Napayok-Short

Illustrated by Jonathan Wright

INHABIT
MEDIA

Akuluk and her stuffed polar bear, Piulua, stepped off the plane. She held on to Piulua while the pilot helped her down the rickety steps that were held up by a thick piece of wire. Akuluk looked up into the bright blue sky. It didn't look much different from the sky in Yellowknife, but Akuluk's mom had told her before they left that she would learn lots of new things when she went to visit her grandparents in Nunavut. Akuluk would have preferred to travel south, to visit her cousin Naala in Montreal, where there were circuses, fairs, rides, and nice new clothes! Her mom had told her that it was important to visit her grandparents, because they had much to show her.

There probably isn't much to do up here, Akuluk thought sadly.

Akuluk and her mom got into an orange taxi van outside the airport. Mom asked the driver to take them to Akuluk's grandma's house. The road they drove down had no pavement at all; it was a long, bumpy, and dusty gravel road to Grandma's house. Along the way, Akuluk spotted big Arctic hares on the side of the road. She had read about them in school and knew what they were. She wondered why they just sat there, looking and seeming like they didn't belong.

The big, rolling hills were green with tiny orange dots.

"Watch out!" exclaimed Akuluk. The taxi swerved to avoid hitting a hare crossing the road.

I wonder what I'm going to see next, Akuluk thought in amazement.

Finally, Akuluk arrived at her grandparents' house. It was the tiniest little blue house that Akuluk had ever seen, sitting at the bottom of a big hill.

Akuluk and her mom entered the house and gave big hugs to her grandma and grandpa.

"Hello, *Anaana* and *Ataata*," Mom said. Akuluk knew that Anaana and Ataata meant Mom and Dad in Inuktitut. She had heard her mom say those words many times, and she liked the idea of calling her grandparents by an Inuktitut name.

Grandma's house was cozy, and it smelled like fresh, sweet bread. On the wall there was a picture of a man with thick, black, curly hair, a crowbar moustache, and a smile. *Could this be why my hair is curly?* Akuluk thought. Her mom's hair and her dad's hair were both straight.

"Who's that, Mommy?" Akuluk asked.

"Oh, that's Ataata when he was young!" laughed Mom.

Akuluk couldn't believe it was the same man who was now standing in front of her grey-haired, thin, and bent over.

"Yes, Akuluk, I was once young like you are now, but that was a looonnng time ago," Ataata chimed in. "Welcome to our house, little one," he said as he gave her a hug. "It's so good to have you here!"

Akuluk and her mom were very tired from their long day of travelling. So, after eating dinner with Ataata and Anaana—Akuluk's favourite part being Anaana's bannock, called *palaugaaq*—Akuluk drifted off to sleep to the lovely, lingering smell of palaugaaq and the distant howls of the neighbour's dog team.

Early the next morning, Akuluk awoke to the lovely scent of Anaana cooking breakfast. When Akuluk shuffled into the kitchen, with Piulua under her arm, she noticed that the eggs Anaana was cooking looked nothing like the eggs she'd seen at home. Some were brightly coloured, others speckled brown, and the yolks were bright orange.

"What are those?" Akuluk asked, curious and a little tentative. Ataata answered, "They're wild eggs that Anaana and I collected from the land. Would you like to pick wild duck eggs with us today? I know a secret island where there are thousands," he said.

Akuluk could not imagine a place that would have thousands of these interesting eggs. A million questions popped into her head, and she blurted out, "Really, Ataata? Where? How far is it? What do I have to wear? Yes, Ataata, I can't wait to go!"

"Not so fast, Akuluk, you must dress for this," said Anaana, as she pulled a fur parka with a huge sunburst trim around the hood out of the closet. "Put this on and the bugs won't bother you. It will keep you nice and snug."

Akuluk donned her beautiful muskrat, wolf, and wolverine fur coat; on the shoulders it had wisps of alternating white and brown fur dangling on the side, and it felt warm and cozy, kind of like her favourite blanket. She felt very grand in it. She wore the warm coat at the table as she quickly ate breakfast, then rushed to the door, ready to go.

Anaana pulled on her waterproof sealskin boots and Ataata put on his old rubber boots. "Don't forget your mitts. Put these on, too!" Anaana said. She had made Akuluk mittens of eider duck skins, which were connected by a long string that she put inside the arms of Akuluk's parka, so she could work and play without dropping her mitts. The mittens were warm and roomy.

"I love my mitts and coat, Grandma," said Akuluk happily. Anaana reminded her that the parka was called an *atigi*. Akuluk showed her mom the beautiful clothes her grandparents had given her.

"Now you're a little Arctic girl in fantastic fashion!" her mom exclaimed.

Ataata laughed and said, "Let's go!"

Ataata started his big, green ATV for the trip. *Vrroom!* The engine came alive and began to vibrate, ready to move. Akuluk put on her helmet and onto the ATV they climbed. Ataata in front, Akuluk in the middle, and Anaana behind her. The ATV carried them up the gravel road in between two muddy ponds. Akuluk turned to wave to her mom one last time before the ATV carried her down another hill.

Akuluk felt the wind against her cheek, but she was sheltered from the cold by Anaana and Ataata. As they rode across the tundra, Akuluk looked out over the lush carpet of spongy, soft, green moss that they travelled on. She did not see a single tree anywhere!

The land was covered with cloudberries—they are called *aqpiit* in Inuktitut, Anaana told her, pointing to the bright orange "raspberry of the North." There were also crowberries—the dark, round, juicy berries known as *paungait* in Inuktitut. Every now and again a spotted brown ptarmigan, with its fluffy, clawed feet, would swoop across the tundra, head bobbing and clucking. Further away, Akuluk spotted a caribou silently, serenely staring at them from a distance; his brown and white fur matched the rocks around him, making him almost invisible.

Finally, the big, green machine slowed to a stop. They were at the Arctic Ocean. Akuluk immediately smelled the beautiful, strong salt sea and the seaweed that floated on the water. She spotted sea clams and scallop shells at the water's edge.

Out in the water, Akuluk saw men in boats. "Hunting beluga," Anaana whispered to Akuluk. Anaana explained that belugas had provided Inuit with a nutritious food, a delicacy called *muktaaq*, for centuries. Akuluk knew this from school, but she liked to hear Anaana explain it to her.

"We must stay quiet now," Ataata told Akuluk. "It's quiet time when we are out here. We stay quiet out of respect for *Piusituqait*, the traditional ways." Ataata pulled a tiny boat into the water from the shore, and, crouching on his knees, he balanced the boat perfectly on the surface. Akuluk had to sit very still in the middle of the boat. Anaana sat motionless at the other end. They had to be very careful to keep everything level and calm on the water. Akuluk was sure that if she moved a muscle, they would tip over and, *splash*—right into the water they'd go! Ataata paddled the boat along, slowly, steadily, and gently.

After a while, Ataata whispered, "Look over there, do you see them? Thousands of birds on the island? That's where we're going. It is called *Munnilik*, or place that has eggs."

Suddenly, there were black and white and brown wings everywhere, birds cawing and crowing, almost filling the sky with their colours. Once in a while, Akuluk saw a king eider with its beautiful emerald green head and bright orange beak.

"That bird is called *mitiq* in our language," Ataata said.

There were also some brown and white birds, eiders and mergansers. The boat landed on the shore of the island, and as they climbed ashore, all the birds flew away in a huge cloud of wings and feathers.

"Wow," said Akuluk, as the birds cleared the island and she saw thousands of nests, all little circles filled with puffy, brown and white down feathers. In some of the nests lay the most beautiful pale turquoise eggs, just as if someone had painted them that way. In one nest, there were brown ones with spots all over them.

"Grandpa, is this one a duck egg?" Akuluk asked.

"Yes, good job, Akuluk! You can tell the difference between wild eggs already. You learn fast. That's a good thing out on the land. Now," he continued, his tone becoming serious, "we have rules when we go hunting and gathering."

"You see this nest with five eggs in it? How about this one with six eggs in it? Here's one with four eggs. We can only take nests with four eggs or fewer, Akuluk. *Piusituqattini,* following traditional ways, means that we can't take nests that have more than four eggs in them. We must leave enough eggs behind for the birds to grow, and for other children in the future to pick, like we are doing now," he said. "A mother bird will leave her nest altogether if she finds even one egg missing. So we must leave some nests completely untouched. Sometimes she will even leave her eggs if she finds they have been handled by humans."

Ataata showed Akuluk how to gather the eggs correctly, so as not to break them. "You have to take the nest itself to use as a cushion for the rest of the eggs," he said.

Akuluk picked only certain nests, just like Ataata said to do. When their bucket was full, Anaana said it was time to go. They got back into the tiny boat and Ataata steered them back to the mainland slowly, steadily, and gently.

At home, Ataata taught Akuluk to put the eggs in water to see which ones they could eat. The eggs that floated to the top of the pot could only be used for baking. The ones that stayed at the bottom of the pot were good for cooking and eating.

Most of them stayed at the bottom. Ataataa said you could only pick eggs at a certain time of year, to make sure they wouldn't float when put in a pot of water. Anaana left the rest of the eggs in the cold porch to use another day.

In the kitchen, Akuluk found a carefully stitched coat wrapped in a red ribbon sitting on her chair at the table. She unwrapped it, and found that was a blue and white *amauti*, just like the one her mother had.

"Now you don't have to worry about carrying Piulua all the time. You can carry him on your back, just like I carried you when you were little," Mom said with a smile.

Akuluk thought it was the most beautiful gift she had ever received.

With Anaana's help, Akuluk put oil in her frying pan and cooked two eggs on the stove. As she sat at the table with her family to eat the best scrambled eggs she had ever tasted, she realized that they tasted even better because she had picked them herself. "Mmmm, I love wild eggs—I mean, I love *munniit*," Akuluk giggled. "And I feel so grown up with my very own amauti!"

At bedtime, Akuluk dreamed of wild ducks and geese, their beautiful pale turquoise eggs, the beautiful brown ones with spots on them, and the two eggs she'd seen with no colours on them at all. They were much, much bigger than the hen eggs she'd been used to seeing in the city. She would be going home soon, but she would come back next summer to go berry picking with Anaana and egg hunting with Ataata.

Maybe someday Akuluk would paddle up to the secret Munnilik island in her own little boat, all by herself. Piulua could come along, too, if he wanted to seek more adventures on the beautiful tundra and the powerful Arctic Ocean.

Inuktitut
Pronunciation Guide

Akuluk (pronounced AH-KOO-LOOK)
name meaning "the loved one"

amauti (pronounced AH-MOW-TI)
an Inuit woman's parka with a pouch in the back used for carrying
babies and small children

Anaana (pronounced A-NAH-NA) Mother

aqpiit (pronounced AQ-PIIT)
cloudberry, sometimes called the "orange raspberry of the North"

Ataata (pronounced A-TAH-TA) Father

atigi (pronounced A-TI-GGI) coat or parka

mitiq (pronounced ME-TIQ) duck, any type

muktaaq (pronounced MUK-TAAQ)
the outer layer of skin of a beluga or narwhal

munniit (pronounced MUH-NIIT) eggs, plural

Munnilik (pronounced MUH-NI-LIK)
name meaning "place with eggs"

palaugaaq (pronounced PA-LA-OO-GAAQ)
bannock, a delicious bread

paungait (pronounced POW-NGAI-EET) crowberries

Piulua (pronounced PEW-LU-AH)
name meaning "the most beautiful"

Piusituqattini (pronounced PEW-SIT-TU-QAT-TEE-NNI)
following traditional or customary ways

Piusuituqait (pronounced PEW-SIT-TU-QA-EET)
traditional or customary ways

Suzie Napayok-Short was born in Frobisher Bay and grew up in Apex, Nunavut, and the DEW Line sites on Baffin Island. She attended residential school before moving to Coral Harbour, Nunavut, and later to Iqaluit, Nunavut. Suzie built a career as an Inuktitut translator and interpreter working for government departments and organizations across Nunavut, the Northwest Territories, and throughout Canada. Suzie currently lives in Yellowknife, Northwest Territories, with her husband, their two children, and one grandchild. She continues her work as a freelance translator and interpreter for businesses across the North. She also works with residential school survivors as an interpreter and guide, helping survivors through the legal process. *Wild Eggs* is Suzie's first book for children. It is inspired by egg-hunting trips she shared with her father.

Jonathan Wright is an illustrator and animator living in Iqaluit, Nunavut. He graduated from Sheridan College in Ontario and has illustrated for a variety of newspapers, magazines, and books. He illustrated *Ava and the Little Folk*, which was shortlisted for the 2014 Silver Birch Express Award.

Iqaluit • Toronto